E Pearson, Susan

Text copyright © 2013 by Susan Pearson
Illustrations copyright © 2013 by Amanda Shepherd
All rights reserved / CIP data is available.
Published in the United States 2013 by
Blue Apple Books, 515 Valley Street, Maplewood, NJ 07040
www.blueapplebooks.com
First Edition 09/13 Printed in Dongguan, China
ISBN: 978-1-60905-050-4

2 4 6 8 10 9 7 5 3 1

MOUSE HOUSE Tales

by Susan Pearson

Illustrated by Amanda Shepherd

BLUE APPLE

MOUSE HOUSE

1

The Right House

"I want a house,"
said Mouse.

"How about a nest?"

"Or a hole
in a tree?"

Home
Sweet
Home

"A high branch is best."

"Oh, no! Not for me!"
said Mouse.
"I'll make my house
beneath this tree."

Home
Sweet
Home

Here Comes Help

"We'll help," said Mole.
"I'm ready to dig.
How many rooms,
and small or big?"

Mouse thought. "Two?
Or three? Or four?"

"No," said Mole.
"You need more!
How about seven?
Or eight?
Or eleven?"

Then Beaver said,
"You need walls and a door.
That's what all this wood is for.
The bark will make
a dandy floor."

Home
Sweet
Home

Goat said,
"I brought cheese.
Let's eat, please."

3

Curtains and Things

"I will spin curtains," said Spider.
"For your windows."

"I brought twigs," said Wren.
"And string.
Just right for nests—
or anything."

"I brought cheese,"
said Goat.

"Can we eat now?"

4

Beds and Chairs

Duck brought feathers
for a bed.
"My very softest ones,"
she said.

"And some of my wool,"
said Sheep.
"For bed covers."

"I brought an egg shell," said Hen.
"It's all I have."

"Fill it with my fur," said Bunny.

"Look! A mouse chair!"

"I brought cheese," said Goat.
"Let's eat now."

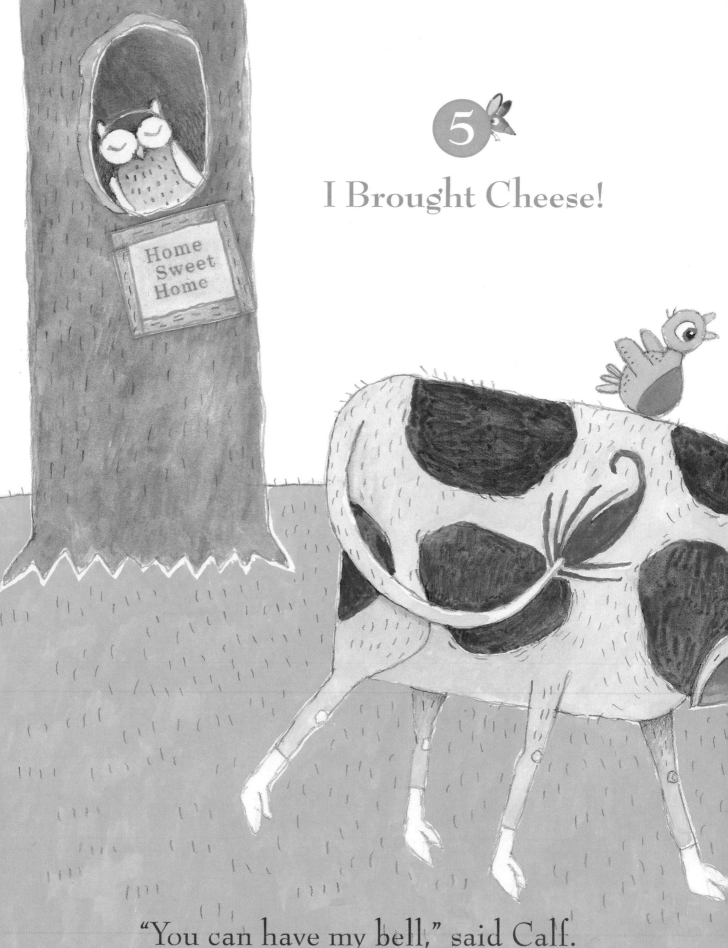

5

I Brought Cheese!

"You can have my bell," said Calf.
"Hang it over your door."

"I brought seeds,"
said Ladybug.
"For a garden."

"We brought honey," said the bees.

Goat said, "I BROUGHT CHEESE!"

"Thank you all," said Mouse.
"For my beautiful house.
Now please have a seat. Let's eat!"

"It's about time!"
said You-Know-Who.

MOUSE MYSTERY

1

Who's There?

Late, late at night,
Mouse heard a sigh,
then a scratch,
then a scrape,
then an odd little cry.

She looked in the closet
and behind the door.
She looked in the cupboard.
She looked in the drawer.

She checked
very carefully
under the chair.

"It must be a ghost,"
said Mouse.
"Who's *there*?"

 2

A Plan

The next day, Mouse told her friends
about the sounds in the night.

"You need a trap," said Wren.

"I'll spin a web," said Spider.
"With any luck,
    the ghost will get stuck."

Bunny said, "I'll bring peas
to spread on the floor.

The ghost will trip
or maybe slip."

"Turn out your lights so the ghost cannot see," said Mole helpfully.

"It won't work," said Goat.

3

Setting the Trap

So that night, Mouse hung the web,
spread the peas, and turned out the light.

And late,
late that night,
Mouse heard a sigh.

Then a scratch.
Then a scrape.

Then an odd
little cry.

Mouse hopped out of bed,
excited to see what she had caught—

but she slipped
on a pea.

She fell into the web
and got stuck like a fly.

"This plan
does not work!"
said Mouse
with a sigh.

4

A New Plan

"I told you so," said Goat the next day.
"For catching a ghost, that's NOT the way."

"Then tell us what is,"
Mouse said to Goat. "Please!"

"Of course," said Goat.
"The best way is CHEESE!"

5

Catching the Ghost

So THAT night,
Mouse put cheese on the table,
and behind the door,

and under the chair,
on her shiny new floor.

Then she hid in the closet,
as quiet as a mouse,

and perked up her ears
to the sounds in her house.

And she heard:

nibble

nibble

nibble

slurp

slibber

slabber

slobber...

BURP!

6
CAUGHT!

Mouse switched on the light.
There in her house was the skinniest,
scraggliest, scruffy young mouse.

His coat was all matted.
He had a black eye.
His whiskers were sticky.
Miss Mouse said, "Oh, my!"

"Please, miss," said the mouse.
"Don't send me away.
I don't have a home.
If you let me stay . . .

I'll wash
your windows . . .

and scrub
your floors . . .

and make
your bed
and paint
your doors
and . . ."

"Calm down!" said Miss Mouse.
"Of course you can stay—

when you've had a bath.
What's your name anyway?"

"Malachi Gimcrack,"
he said. "Call me Mack."

7

A Happy Ending

Such a snug little house
for two mice together,
in rain and in shine—
in all kinds of weather.

Old friends and new friends
come over to play,

and this mystery ends
with a party—HOORAY!

"Put it on crackers,
put it on bread,

cheese goes best
with friends,"
Goat said.

THE END

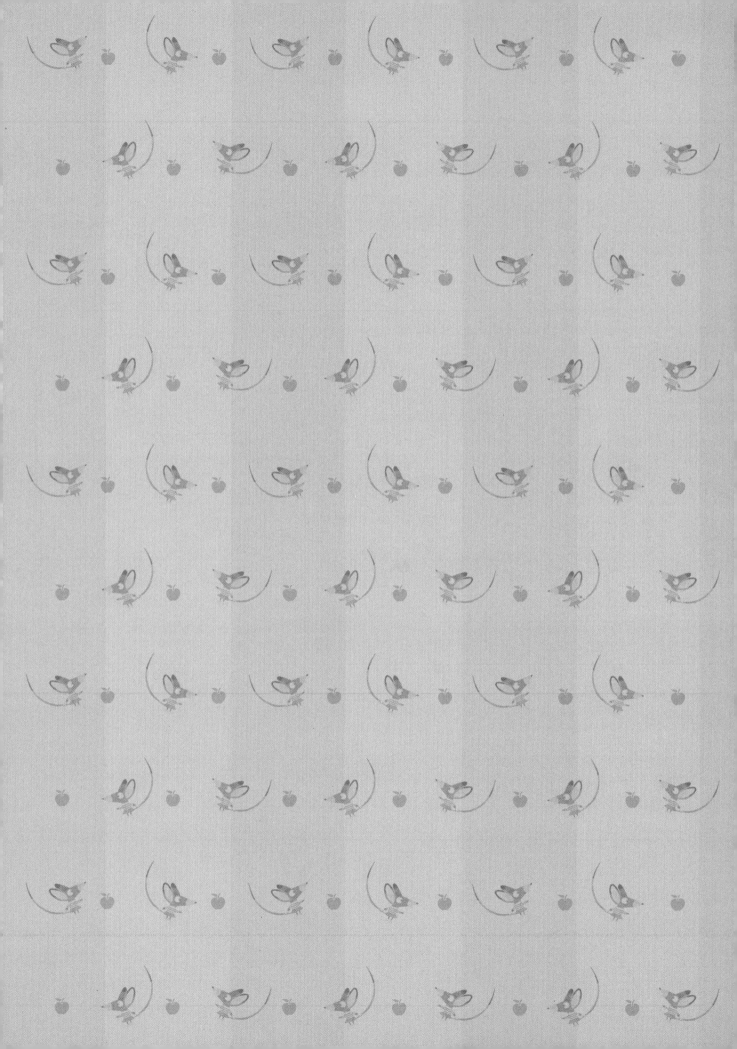